I Like You just Because

Thoughts on FRIENDSHIP

ALBERT J. NIMETH
O.F.M.

FRANCISCAN HERALD PRESS

Dedicated To
JOE & ROSE CICHOSZEWSKI
JOE & JOSEPHINE GOGOL

FRANCISCAN HERALD PRESS
1434 WEST 51st STREET ● CHICAGO, 60609

INTRODUCTION

"I'll get by with a little help from my friends."
No one appreciates the truth of that statement
more than I. It takes a lot of people to pub-
lish a book. This one is no exception. I owe
so much to the people who have entered my
life and who have allowed me to enter theirs.
In the process we experienced budding
friendships. Some of them matured; some
wilted but all left their mark. This book is
offered with the hope that some of the di-
mensions of friendship will be better ap-
preciated.

I am especially grateful to the members of
the youth groups of the third order of St.
Francis. They have taught me so much by the
friendships they offer. By allowing me to
share in their lives they have given me more
than they will ever know.

In particular for special services I want to
thank Jan for the cover design and graffiti,
Roger and George for photography, Paula
for the banner designs, Arlene, "Sarah,"
"Charlie," Lydia and Rita for picture and
text suggestions.

A. J. N.

LIKE A GUST OF WIND A FRIENDSHIP HAS SHAKEN ME

paula

PREFACE

Friendship is
a happy thing.
It makes us
laugh.
It makes us
sing.
It makes us
sad.
It makes us
cry.
It makes us seek
the reason why.
It makes us
take.
It makes us
give.
Above all else
it makes us
LIVE.

Pensive, withdrawn
lonely.
The life of the world
can be
teeming around us:
the high decibel sounds
can be dinning
in our ear
and still
we can be
lonely.

A person
can be lonely
in a multiple family dwelling
where the
slightest sound
is heard
next door.

It is possible
to be lonely
in a crowd.

Loneliness haunts
the places
where
crowds gather.

It is not
the presence or
absence
of people
that makes
the difference
because a person
need not
be lonely
even if he is
alone.

Sometimes it is good
to be
alone.
But that
does not make us
lonely.

It is not a matter
of being
present with someone.
It is a matter
of being
present to someone.

This kind of presence
has the ability
to let the being
of the other
come through
to me, here and now.
This means
acceptance of myself
and acceptance
of him.
It means,
in a way,
assuming responsibility
for him and
my actions
toward him.

This calls for
special communication,
special human interaction,
special acceptance and
understanding.

If these are lacking,
all we have is a juxta-position
of lonely people,
each encased within

his own
impenetrable shell.

The pity is
lonely people
are unhappy.

If their thoughts
turn inward,
as they often do,
they demean
their own worth.

They tend
to exaggerate
their deficiencies.
What is worse,
they tend
to identify
with
their deficiencies.

They lose
confidence and
self-esteem.
Without these
life
is unbearable.

If their thoughts
turn outward,
they become embittered
because they
interpret
their isolation
as a rejection
by others.

They bristle
with ill-will
because they feel
terribly threatened.

One of their defenses
is to become
obnoxious
so people will keep
their distance.
In this way
there is less risk
of harm
by exposure.

They alienate
the very thing
they want
and need—people.

No one wants
to be lonely.
No one
needs to be doomed
to a life
of loneliness.

It is possible to
BREAK OUT !

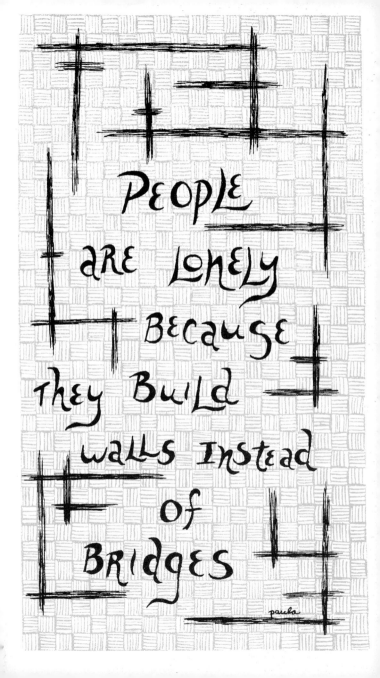

To dissolve
loneliness
we need friends.

A true friend
brings joy
into life.

He pours back
into a soul
his self-respect.

FRIENDSHIP
WARMS THE
HEART

A friend
    inspires
    encourages
    gives heart to grow
    helps to think more kindly
        to live more graciously.

A friend
  gives warmth
    understanding,
    time
    love
    himself.
A friend
  stands up to my anger
    my selfishness
    my short-comings.
A friend
  walks with me
  works with me
  cries with me
  laughs with me.

Sacred Scripture:
   "A fragrant oil
gladdens the heart
as friendship's sweetness
comforts the soul."

"A faithful friend
is a sure shelter.
Whoever finds one
has found
a rare treasure."

"A faithful friend is
something
beyond price.
There is
no measuring
his worth."

"A faithful friend
is an elixir of life."

V.C.ANDERSON

NOBODY LOVES ME

"Nobody loves me. I'm going into the garden to eat worms.
Yesterday I ate two smooth ones and one woolly one."

"Nobody loves me.
I'm going to go out
and eat
some worms."

This strikes us
as humorous.
But it is
deep tragedy.

The child
is telling us
something about
an intense human need
that is
not being satisfied.

Because it is
not being satisfied,
there is
a sense
of worthlessness.

This is deep tragedy.

In his inimitable way
I suppose
Snoopy
would cut thru
to the core and say:
"Happiness
is a friend
who lets you
be yourself
and still
loves you."

To maintain
our peace of mind
and the
proper perspective
we need
at least
one good friend.

We need someone
in whose presence
we can
be our ugly selves
without having to worry
about the image
we create.

We need someone
in whose presence
we can
let our hair down,
kick off our shoes
and be
our true selves
without camouflage or
pretense.
We don't have to
keep up a front
because
a true friend
will not keep us
in a
moral straitjacket.

With him
we can
let it all
hang out.

We all need someone
who will
accept us
without question,
who will

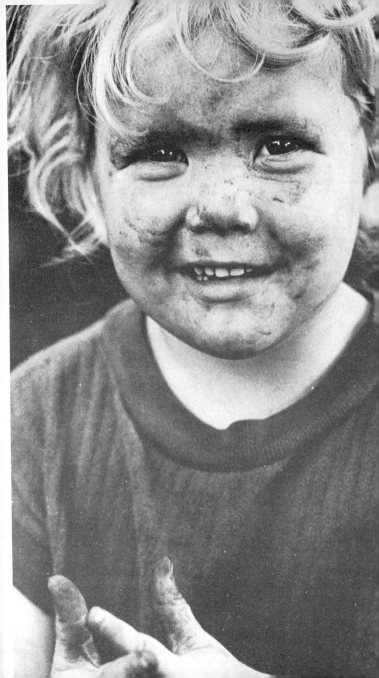

love us—
"just because."

We need friends
because we are
social beings,
not by choice,
but by nature.

It is unnatural
to live
sealed off
from the rest of man.

Put a man
in solitary confinement too long
and he will
go mad.

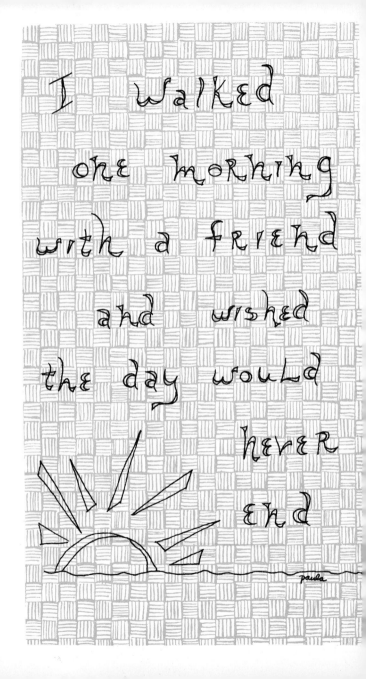

A mark of a
genuine friendship
is the privilege of
being yourself
and still
being accepted.

A true friendship
always tells us that
we are
acceptable and
accepted.
This we all
need to know.

We have a need
to be accepted
not for
any special quality,
not for
any grand achievement
but simply
for ourselves.

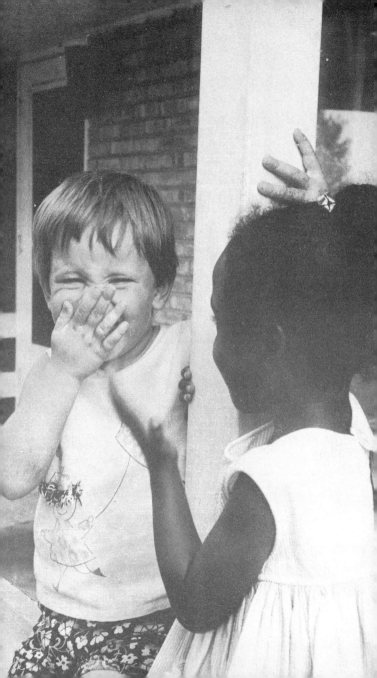

A great deal of
personal dissatisfaction
and discontent
sets in
when we think
poorly of ourselves
because we do not feel
accepted by others.

We are most miserable
when we
doubt ourselves and
think we are inadequate.

The opinion
we have of ourselves
is often a reflection
of the opinion
we think others
have of us.

Tension sets in
when we strain to be pleasing
and accepted
on terms other than
being ourselves.

A friend
relieves that strain
because he tells us
we do not have to be
anything
other than what we really are.

As we experience
acceptance
in a friendship,
we come to know that
someone sees value
in us.
Being valued
by someone who counts
is the first step
toward valuing oneself.

Accepting a friend
as he is
is not to give him
a license
to be ugly,
mean and
despicable.

Acceptance
gives a friend
support
but it also
challenges him
to become
what he can become—
a noble,
fine person.

Along life's road I found a friend who brought
    me joys untold
A happiness to fill my heart more valuable than
    gold
A dream of bigger things to come, a friend, a
    faith, a smile.
Along life's road I found them all to make my
    life worthwhile.

If a person
is understood
accepted and loved,
he will grow
as a person.

But understanding
is deeper than
knowledge.

There are many people
who know us,
but very few
who understand us.

Understanding
is more
of the heart
than of the mind.

All that we love deeply

becomes a part of us.

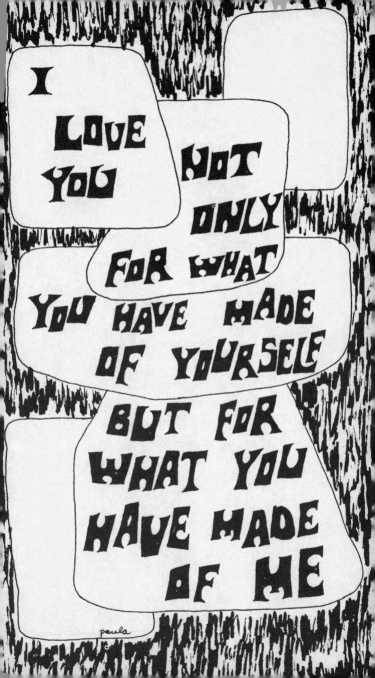

5 When a dog
recognizes the footsteps
of his master,
he begins to caper, dance
and wag everything behind his ears.
He wants to leap
out of his skin
to let his master know
how glad he is
to see him.
With this kind of
enthusiastic "hello"
who can
resist him?
You simply must
be his friend
because he lets you know
so emphatically
that he wants to be yours.

A dog teaches
a valuable lesson.

We cannot sit back
and expect
friendships
to happen.

Seeds of friendship
will take root
only if the soil
is properly prepared.

If we go thru life
like an accident
looking for a place to happen,
people will give us
wide berth.
They will
avoid us.

FRIENDSHIP
TICKLES A FUNNYBONE

TEACHER

PRIVATE

When a person offers
his hand
in friendship,
he does so
with misgivings.
He is not sure
that his overtures
of friendship
will be accepted.

If he senses rejection,
the offer is
withdrawn
instinctively and
immediately.
If he senses
an openness,
a willingness
to gamble with his offer,
he too is willing
to continue
to take the chance.

To encourage friendships
we have to
extend ourselves.
We have
to let people know that
we are open
to their offers
of friendship.

A person who complains
that he has
no friends,
will do well
to study his demeanor.

A chilly "leave me alone" attitude
is hardly calculated
to invite friendship.

We cannot
single out
any particular feature
and say
this
invites friendship.
It has to do
with the total person.
It works
in many subtle ways.

If we want
a friendly response,
we have to show that
we are friendly.

*We must see ourselves
and our love as a gift
to the other.
We offer but we
do not know
if it will be accepted.*

Friendship
is a two-way street.
If it is not fed
from both sides,
it will atrophy.

"Why do I
always have to make
the phone calls?
How come
you never call me?"
This kind of complaint
is a bad omen.
Corrosion has set in,
because there is
no real exchange.

We have to
have time
for our friends.
We must be
available.

It is so easy
to plead
a multitude of demands
on our time.

How important are
these "demands?"
If a friendship
is to thrive,
we have to face
this question because
a friendship
cannot survive
neglect.

Being available means
to take the initiative.
Write that letter,
make the phone call,
stop for a visit
even if it isn't your turn.

Being available means
altering plans
to accommodate

Being available means
to listen
not only to what
our friend is saying
but what
he is not saying
or trying to say
and cannot.

Sometimes we are unavailable
because
we are afraid
of getting hurt.
So we withdraw
to our tower,
fill the moat, and
pull up
the drawbridge.

This fear is there
but we have to cope
with it.
We have to be willing
to suffer
the agony of opening
to others.

We have to let down
the bridge,
open the gate.
Soon we will discover
that people will
treat us gently.
We have to risk it.

More than anything
we have to realize
we cannot
drain the cup of friendship,
taking all we can get
of care, attention and
concern
without doing our share
to help refill
the cup.

Friendship is a golden chain made stronger with
    each year
Each link is forged of memories that make you
    still more dear
The thoughtful things you say and do become
    the links of gold
That I will treasure through the years and in my
    heart will hold.

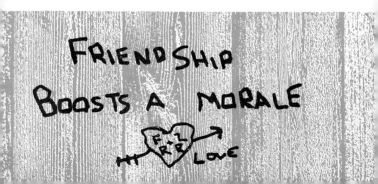

I'll get by with a little

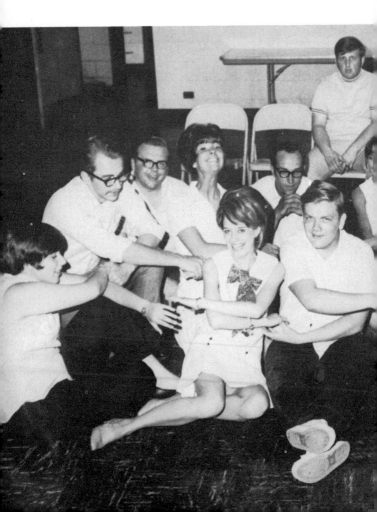

help from my friends

7 I remember
hating a professor
for a strange reason.
He would not let me
do anything for him.
If I opened the door for him,
he shoved me thru.
If I offered
to be of service,
he turned me down
with some snide remark
about not being helpless.
He was smug
and self-sufficient.
He needed
nothing from me.
And I hated him.
Why?
I had a need
to be needed.
He frustrated
that need.

To have friends
we need humility.

A person who is
so full of himself
that there is
no room for anyone else
in his life
will go thru life
friendless.

We cannot build
friendships
by towering
over others.
We have to get down
from our high horse
of pride and
self-centeredness
and meet people
on ground level.

A proud and
selfish person
finds it impossible
to see value
in another person—
any value or importance
that is meaningful
to him.
If he cannot see this,
he cannot
enter into a
genuine friendship,
because
when we extend
the palm of friendship,
we are telling someone:

"You are important to me.
You bring
new value
into my life."

Friends need to be needed.
We have to allow
our friends
to be of service.
This does not mean
we can become
overbearing
in our demands
on his time
and talent.
But it does mean
we must
graciously accept
whatever services
he wants to render.

There is no comfort
or solace
in my gifts and talents
unless
there is someone
who needs me.

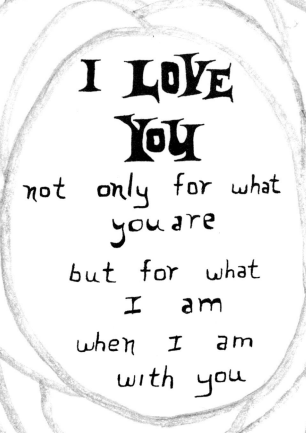

I LOVE YOU

not only for what
you are

but for what
I am
when I am
with you

Friendships are dangerous
and threatening
because they make us
want to reveal ourselves.

Friends want to know
and be known.
A friendship, in fact,
grows
as friends get to know
each other better.

This goes to the core
of one's personality.
This self-revelation
is not easy
to come by.
It is risky.
However, because a friendship
creates an atmosphere
of love and trust
we are willing
to risk
revealing ourselves.
The climate is right

and the opportunity safe.
The mere fact
of not being forced
to put on a front
inclines us
to expose ourselves
in a deeper manner.

There is a continuing discovery
as we reveal
new layers of ourselves
to each other.

This opens
new horizons,
elicits
greater awareness,
deepens feeling and
adds meaning
to life.

When we permit ourselves
to be known in depth,
we expose ourselves
not only to
a friend's balm
but to an enemy's bomb.

Because of the
deep self-disclosure
in a friendship
it is imperative
that friends
be loyal.

The revelation of
personal intimacies
is a sacred trust.
Often the happiness
of a lifetime
is riding on them.

This trust
must never
be betrayed.
It is given in confidence
and must be
guarded with loyalty.

When a confidence
is betrayed
something fine and
beautiful dies.

Emptiness sets in.
The betrayed
begins to doubt
his worth.
If friends
prove untrue
what is there
to live for?

Because there is
so much
poured into a friendship,
all the more reason
for loyalty.

Loyalty is the price
we must pay
for offering and
accepting friendship.
This is written into
the very nature
of the relationship and
cannot be taken lightly.

In every genuine friendship
we have

a right to expect and
an obligation
to give loyalty.

No matter
what the secrets
I entrust to you
they still remain
a part of me
and cannot
be violated.

9 "I've got him
all figured out.
I really have his number.
If you want to know
anything about him,
just ask me."
This smugness is
damaging
to a friendship.

Friends are not things
to be labeled, catalogued
and card-punched.

Friends are not
crossword puzzles
to be
figured out.

Friends are
people
to be loved.

The moment you
put a friend
in a certain category,
you put him in a
straitjacket.
You swindle him
of some of
his liberty.

Once you pass judgement
on a friend,
he is
congealed.
He can no longer
grow.

No matter what he does
after that
it is twisted
and distorted
until it comes to focus
under the glasses
of prejudgement.

Nobody has the right
to curtail
one's freedom

to change
to grow
to be.

A friendship
must always allow
room to grow.

When we categorize,
we attempt
to dominate.
No friend
has the right
to dominate another.

Liberty must remain
intact.
Why?
A friendship
increases self-esteem
which gives
a greater incentive
to develop.
Therefore
friends must be free
to be fully
what they are
and what
they can become.

Friendships also
carry the challenge
to measure up
to great expectations.

If I am pegged,
catalogued and slotted,
I am
hemmed in and
hamstrung.

My desire
to strive for higher goals
must not be stifled.

No matter
how beautiful your sound
may be,
I must be free
to march
to the beat
of my own drums.

A friendship
cannot be
jealous and possessive.

A relationship
that turns in on itself
becomes selfish and
stultifying.

A friend
ought not
engage another so completely
that his gifts
and talents
are not available
to others.

We need the freedom
to share ourselves
with others.

I do my thing, and you do your thing.
I am not in the world to live
   up to your expectations
And you are not in this world
   to live up to mine.
You are you and I am I
And if by chance we find each other,
   it's beautiful.

                              —F. S. Perls

10 I stood in front of a
trick mirror.
When I struck a
George Atlas pose,
I was transformed into
Mr. America!

How corny!
How phony!
I wouldn't
dare buy a suit
on the basis
of what I saw
in a trick mirror.

If I buy a suit,
I had better buy it
on the basis of
what is really there;
not what
I imagine
to be there.

When I look deeper
into myself,
I find I am still prone
to stand
in front of
trick mirrors.

It is so easy
to find
more than is there or
better than
the reality.

This is phony.
And this is why
I find it hard
to grow.
But grow I must
or decay.

A good friend
can be a great help
in removing
trick mirrors.
To do so
he must be honest
with me.

If I am to grow,
I must deal with
the real me.
A friend
who honestly
tells me

what he observes and
how he evaluates what he sees
is doing me
a great service.
He is a true friend.

If I rely
on my own judgement,
I am apt to be
wide of the mark.
The honest opinion
of a trusted friend
is invaluable.

It is difficult
to face the truth
about oneself.
The job becomes easier
if the truth
comes from a friend.

He sees us
as we appear
to others.
We do not have this
perspective
but it is a
perspective we need.

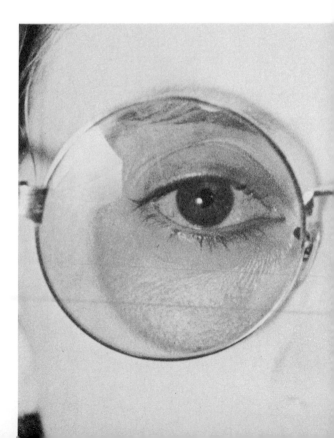

A friend
can be trusted
not to blurt out
everything
that comes to mind.
He will know
the fitness

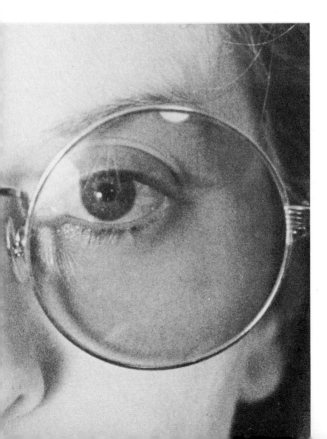

of time and place.
He will know how
to temper
with tact
without diluting the truth.
Because he is
a friend
he will know how
to deal with us.
He will respect
our feelings
because he understands.
He will not dissimulate or
camouflage.
He will know that
the last thing we need
is flattery or
dishonesty.
He will know that
if he does not
level with us
we end up
in front of a
trick mirror.

This is
no basis for growth.

FRIENDSHIP NEEDS NO WORDS.

IT IS

SOLITUDE

DELIVERED FROM

THE

ANGUISH

OF LONELINESS.

" We must
share ourselves
because
our hearts are
so big and strong.

We must
seek the support
of others
because
our hearts are
so small and weak.

This is the paradox
we all
must live with.

No one ever
remains stagnant.
As a human person
we are
forever becoming.
We grow daily.
This is why
we must continue
to share.

*If I cannot understand
my friend's silence,
I will never understand
his words.*

You tell me
who you are and
I tell you
who I am.

If I can hear you
and you can
hear me
with the same freshness and
awareness,
the same
wonder and joy,
as in the beginning,
our friendship
will take deeper roots.

There have been moments
in our lives
when we were
so full of joy
we felt we would burst
unless
we shared it with someone.

Zorba had to share
the joy of life
by dancing.

A newly published author
wanted to share
his joyous news,
only to discover that
no one really cared
if he published or not.
How sad.

There have been moments
in our lives
when we ached
to the bottom of our being,
longing for someone
to listen and understand
without putting us down as a
chronic complainer.

*There is nothing
so bitter
as the bitterness
of suffering alone*

Among the privileges
of friendship
is the opportunity
to share
some of the deeper feelings
of human life—
the joys and sorrows.

Whatever happens to us
a friend must know.
We do not trust ourselves
to read an event correctly
unless his eye
reads and interprets
with us.

Pain is lessened
when shared
with a friend
who cushions the blow.

Joys are doubled
when shared
with a friend.
Then two hearts are happy.
Two people
laugh and sing.

When stopped up
with emotion
because of insult or injury,
real or imaginary,
it is difficult
to think straight.
We warp and torture
our normal feelings
and thoughts.

Sharing the feeling
with a friend
will prevent us
from wallowing
in fantasies of revenge.

A friend
is for sharing.

Sharing our thoughts,
our fears,
our complaints
clears the mind
for more sensible action.

No matter what the turmoil
everything

can come out
in the presence
of a friend.

This will prevent
an outburst
in a place and
at a time
that would be
unjustifiable and
unsafe.

All this
because a friend
knows
how to listen.

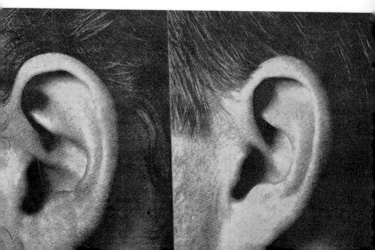

It is no disgrace
to share
our troubles.
It is no crime
to need sympathy
and understanding
of friends.

In a friendship
there is
the magical warmth
of the human heart
that surpasses
the power of medicine.

*A friend hears the song
in my heart
and sings it to me
when my memory fails.*
—Athena

"To live with saints in heaven
is full of bliss and glory.
To live with saints on earth
is quite a different story."

If it takes
a lot of character
to live with the saints,
it takes all the more
to live
with friends,
for one of the
continuing demands
of friendship is
forbearance.

We need forbearance
not because
our demands are great
and insistent
but because our moods
are forever shifting.
Like the phases of the moon
our moods
are regular in their inconstancy.

Sudden and frequent
changes of mood
affect the brightness
of life within
and put a strain
on the people
around us.
This is why
forbearance
must be in generous supply.
A friend has to be ready
to cope
with every changing mood.
He has to know
how to be gracious
and soothing.
He has to be able
to hear out
our one-sided story
for the hundredth time.
He has to know
how to relieve
the pain and
quiet the hurt
with that gentle touch
that knows
how to heal.

If we are
Ever
to love a
Butterfly
we must first
care for a few
caterpillars

A nasty mood or
a burst of temper
will not turn him sour.
He understands
how little it takes
to affect a person—
            a slight annoyance,
            a press of work,
            a preoccupation.
So he will wait.
This too will pass.

Forbearance calls for
discipline and
self-control.

Since friendship is
the free bestowal
of one person
on another,
it can be achieved only
by someone
who is so much
in control of himself
that he is able
to give himself freely.

It takes a lot of
self-discipline
to bear with others
when we ourselves
may be in need
of the same understanding.

It takes discipline
to wait our turn.

But right now
"as long as he needs me"
I will try to be on hand
and helpful.

If he needs
my strength,
I will try to be
strong.

If he needs
my understanding,
I will try to
understand.

If he needs
my patience,
I will try to be
long-suffering.

If he needs
my love,
I will
give without stint.

I belong
where I am needed.

A friend is
one who knocks
before he enters
not after he leaves.

Whether I am
with him or away from him
I owe a friend
respect and
appreciation.

St. Thomas:
"A friendship requires
that a person wish another
the good he wishes himself,
so that
he desires to converse with him
and share with him
those aspects of life
that he
especially values."

Our hunger
for appreciation is
legitimate and
sound.

A friendship tries
to supply
this need.

To appreciate means
to set a value on,
to esteem fully.
It means to be
grateful
for what a person is;
to treasure him
precisely as a person—
as the person
he truly is.

To appreciate a friend means
to recognize
his gifts and talents,
to be happy
he has them,
to want him
to develop them
to the fullest,
to encourage him
to use his talents
in every possible way.
We will never
look upon his success
as a threat
to our self-esteem.

If necessary
we will help him
recognize and
utilize his talents
and gifts.
We will encourage him
to be successful and
reach his potential.

The
greatest good
you can do
for another
is not just to
share
your Riches,
but to
Reveal to him
his
own

paula

We appreciate a friend
when we give him
more than
the usual routine treatment.

If he is special,
we show it
by the manner in which
we treat him.

Even in the intimacies
that develop
in a friendship
we will always
be sensitive to his feelings.
We will avoid anything
that can be construed
as a lack of
respect and appreciation.

When disagreements arise,
as they will,
friends can disagree
without resorting
to hurt and harm,
without sacrificing
mutual esteem and
appreciation.

If disagreements
get out of hand,
a real friend
will make the first move
toward reconciliation.

When the occasion arises,
a friend will be there
to extend compliments and
congratulations,
to share our joy.
He will take sincere delight
in acknowledging
our accomplishments.

The great and
wonderful things
we expect to gain
from a friendship
point up
the great and
wonderful things
we must
bring to a friendship.

Somehow friends always
continue to live with us
in us and
through us.

I LIKE YOU!

I like you
And I know why,
I like you because
You are a good person to like.
I like you because
When I tell you something special
You know it's special
And you remember it
A long, long time.
You say,
"Remember when you told me
something special?"
And both of us remember.
When I think something is important,
You think it's important too.
We have good ideas.
When I say something funny, you laugh.
I think I'm funny.
You think I'm funny too.
I like you because
You know where I'm ticklish

And you don't tickle me there
Except just a tiny bit . . .
Sometimes.
Stop!
But if you do, then I know where
to tickle you too.
You know how to be silly.
That's why I like you.
Boy! Are you ever silly!
I never met anyone sillier than me
Till I met you.
I like you because
You know when it's time to stop
being silly.
Maybe day after tomorrow.
Maybe never.
Oops! Too late!
It's quarter past silly.
We fool around the same way all the time.
Sometimes we don't say a word.
We snurkle under fences,
We spy secret places.
If I'm a goofus on the roofus,
You are one too.
If I pretend I'm drowning,
You pretend you're saving me.
If I am getting ready to pop a paper bag,

Then you are ready to jump.
That's because you really like me.
You <u>really</u> like me, don't you?
And I like you back.
And that's the way we keep going
Everyday . . .
If I go away, then you go away.
Or if I stay home,
You send me a postcard.
You just don't say
Well, see you around sometime.
Bye.
I like you a lots because of that.
If we go away together
And if I get lost in Grand Central Station,
Then you are the one that's yelling
for me:
Hey, where are you?
Here I am.
I like you because
When I am feeling sad
You don't cheer me up right away.
Sometimes it's better to be sad.
You can't stand others being
so googly and goggly
Every single moment.
You want to know about things.

It takes time.
I like you because
If I am mad at you
Then you get mad at me too.
It's awful when the other person isn't.
Phooey!
They are just so nice and so hoo-hoo you
could just punch them in the nose.
I like you because
When I think I am going to throw up
You don't pretend you are busy
Looking at the birds and all that.
You say: "Maybe it was something
you ate."
You say: "That happened to me one time."
And the same thing did.
If you find two four leaf clovers,
You give me one.
If I find four, I give you two.
If we find only three, we keep looking.
Sometimes we have good luck
And sometimes we don't.
If I break my arm and if you break your
arm too,
Then it is lots of fun to have a
broken arm.
You tell me about mine

And I tell you about yours.
We both are sorry.
We write names and draw pictures.
We show everybody and they wish they
had broken arms too.
I like you because—I don't know why—
but—
Everything that happens is nicer with you.
I can't remember when I didn't like you.
It must have been lonesome then.
I like you because—because—because—
It's the fourth of July
On the fifth of July.
And if you and I had some drums
And some horns and horses and some
fire engines,
We could be a holiday
We could be a celebration
We could be a whole parade.
See what I mean?
Even if it was the nine hundredth and
ninety-ninth of July
Even if it was August
Even if it was way down at the bottom
of November
Even if it was no place in particular
in January

110

I would go on choosing you
And you would go on choosing me
Over and over again.
That's how it would happen every time.
I don't know why.
I guess I don't know <u>why I really</u>
like you.
Why do I like you? ? ?
I guess I like you- - -
I guess I like you- - -
Because I LIKE YOU.

—Sandol Stoddard Warburg*

*Used with permission of
Houghton Mifflin Company
Boston, Massachusetts

Photo credits:

Roger Diamond: Pages 13, 20, 53, 69, 102, 104

George Kroeck: Pages 50-51, 81, 91

Algimantas Kezys, S.J.: Pages 11, 19, 39, 47, 67, 73, 83, 85, 86

Jean-Claude LeJeune: Pages 26, 30-31, 45, 76-77

Ken Feil: Page 35

J. Ballard: Page 41

John Padula, Maryknoll: Page 55

Louis Millette: Page 9

Any infringement of copyrights is unintentional and will be rectified in subsequent editions if called to the attention of the publisher.